A Very Ghostly Christmas

An Anthology of Seasonal Ghost Stories

Edited by A.R. Ward

A Very Ghostly Christmas

A Ghost Orchid Press Anthology

First published in Great Britain 2022 by Ghost Orchid Press

ISBN (paperback): 978-1-7396116-0-6

ISBN (e-book): 978-1-7396116-1-3

Cover design © Claire L. Smith

Book formatting by Claire Saag

"There must be something ghostly in the air of Christmas – something about the close, muggy atmosphere that draws up the ghosts, like the dampness of the summer rains brings out the frogs and snails."

— *Jerome K. Jerome,* Told After Supper

Contents

Foreword by Sara Crocoll-Smith 7

It's Later Than You Think by R.L. Summerling................ 9

Red Satin and Pearls by Sharmon Gazaway 13

The Shades of Midwinter by Andrew Lyall..................... 17

A Cardinal Sin by Lori Green 21

Warm Hands, Cold Bones by April Yates 25

The Man Who Hated Christmas by Eleanor Sciolistein... 29

The Dead Come at Christmas by Maggie Nerz Iribarne.. 33

House of Whispers by Warren Benedetto 37

The Locked Door by Sally Hughes 41

The Full Cold Moon by Alex Ebenstein 45

Dreadful Things by Nicole Little 49

Bone Kindling by Sophia DeSensi.................................. 53

Die Kleine Weihnachtmaus by J. L. Royce 57

Escher's Tree House by SJ Townend 61

Do You See What I See? by Jessica McHugh 65

The Man of the House by Rebecca Jones-Howe 69

A Victorian Secret by Jay Seate....................................... 73

Some Ghosts are Made by Vivian Kasley........................ 77

The Deserter by Anthony Engebretson............................ 81

Spirit of the Seasons by Marisca Pichette....................... 85

Mr Swill's Generosity by Scotty Sarafian 89

The Boy in the Lake by Alice Austin 93

Beckwith House by Samantha Arthurs 97

Hunger by Olivia Graves 101

Sea Grave by Danielle Edwards.................................... 105

Laid Out in Lavender by Leila Martin 109

Sister Agnes by H.B. Diaz 113

The Bodegraven Man by Clyde Davis 117

Foreword

Sara Crocoll Smith

The tradition of telling ghost stories during Christmastime began before written records and can be found in cultures around the world. As the days grow short and our shadows grow long, we huddle close together by the fire and contemplate--the time behind us, the loved ones present and those lost, and the new year ahead.

This cozy, dark time of year provides room in our lives to spin spooky tales and do our level best to frighten each other for fun. So, in fall of 2021, when Antonia asked me if I would like to team up with Ghost Orchid Press and judge "A Very Ghostly Christmas" flash fiction contest, I was completely on board.

Each entry was delightfully creepy, and it was incredibly difficult to pick the winning entries and runners up. Amongst the stellar stories featured in this haunting holiday anthology, you'll find:

- 1st place winner: "The Bodegraven Man" by Clyde Davis
- 2nd place winner: "It's Later Than You Think" by R.L. Summerling
- 3rd place winner: "Sister Agnes" by H.B. Diaz
- Runner up: "Red Satin and Pearls" by Sharmon Gazaway
- Runner up: "The Shades of Midwinter" by Andrew Lyall

I'm excited for you to experience these chilling works of fiction for yourself. Dim the lights, cuddle up with this book, and savor the ghastly ghost stories contained within. Happy holidays!

Sincerely,
Sara Crocoll Smith
Publisher / Editor-in-Chief
Love Letters to Poe

It's Later Than You Think

R.L. Summerling

Sweat clung to me beneath the crimson velvet of my dress. I marvelled at the coolness of your skin, your slim manicured fingers laced with mine. A woman in a mountainous snowy wig entered the stage and began trilling about love, I think. You were a distraction, causing me to lose the thread of the plot some time ago. It was New Year's Eve and the cloak of the new century was closing in. Filled with recklessness, I had suggested we go to the opera; why shouldn't we be seen together in public?

"Here," you'd said with a glint of diablerie in your eye, "let me."

As you dripped laudanum under my tongue, I found exquisite delight in our shared perversion. The actress finished her aria and you gave me a smeared lipstick smile, one that matched my giddiness, with no trace of that demure woman you were around your husband. The chandeliers blazed too brightly and the edges of my vision began to blur, my head lolled forward.

You squeezed my hand twice sharply; the pinch of bones touching made me snap my head up. I blinked rapidly to try to sober myself, a trick I had tried ever since I drained my first decanter of wine when I was thirteen years old. That's when I noticed him. The man in the box directly opposite us, with high cheekbones and an aquiline nose that matched mine.

"Father," I said.

It couldn't be; my father was dead. I had watched as the fever had wracked his body, stripping him of the dignity and morals he held so dear. His demise had been agonizing and slow, the medicine he had dedicated his life to brought little relief. Now he sat before me as I remembered him in those final days, more of death than life. His skin was pallid and he was shrouded in a dark heavy cloth. Milky eyes were sunken deep into his skull and his lips, cracked and thin, had receded over his gums. My stomach contorted with fear and I wanted to scream for your help, but I could make no sound.

The spectre of my father held out a skeletal hand and I saw in his palm he held a pocket watch. The silver glinted in the candlelight and all at once, I became terrified of both the past and the future. If only this opera would never end, the clock would never strike midnight, and you wouldn't return to your husband.

I pushed my way out of the packed theatre and stumbled into the cold night air, my breath coming hard and fast. I tried to compose myself, but dread filled me as I felt a hand on my shoulder, icy fingertips against my neck. I let out a cry and whipped around; expecting to see the ghost of my father, but it was you. Red and gold sparks rained over the city; the New Year's Eve fireworks had already begun.

R.L. SUMMERLING is a writer from South East London. In her free time she enjoys befriending crows in Nunhead Cemetery. You can find her at rlsummerling.com.

Red Satin and Pearls

Sharmon Gazaway

He strides in, and a shiver runs down my tightly laced back. Framed in the parlor's gaslight, he is not tall; too stocky to be elegant. He takes the liberty of pinching and sniffing the cedar garland draping the archway. He surveys the room with a glance that annoyingly conveys ownership, and fondles a red satin sash tied about his waist.

Clearly, he's been here before. I know this man—somehow.

The room hums with our guests' hushed conversation around the crystal punch bowl, their heads bent in some bit of gossip.

I rise from the divan, and my brother joins me.

I touch my pearl choker, my breath constricted. "Giles, who is that man?"

"Who do you mean?" He gazes about the room, eyes blank.

"Him. The coarse one."

He smiles patiently. "Come, Sister. Let's sit by that lovely fire. I'm quite chilled."

Giles coughs, and eases a finger between his cravat and ashen throat, exposing an ugly bruise.

"Alice, you've gone quite pale," he says, brows pinched together.

"I—I'm fine." But the room seems to lurch, the chandelier's gas flames mere shadows of themselves.

The stranger looks up sharply at the large portrait of Giles and me above the mantel. His face is filled with … gloating?

As he strides toward us, I raise my chin, square my shoulders. Yet he brushes past us as if we don't exist, the bay rum scent of his hair tonic sickeningly familiar.

"My dear new friends," he says, "raise a glass to the new owner of Brantley Hall. You are very welcome. Enjoy the cheer of the season and many happy returns." He lifts his glass high, and tips it ever so slightly toward our portrait.

New owner? Not only is he coarse, but presumptuous and rude. As if we'd ever part with Brantley.

The trussed and starched crowd raise their cups; few sip.

"Such poor taste," whispers a tall whiskered man.

"You'd think he'd at least remove the portrait," his young wife murmurs.

The coarse man wraps the red satin sash 'round his hand absently, like a talisman, oblivious to the gossip.

"They never found him, you know," says the wife's friend. "They searched and searched. The man is still at large."

Glancing at our portrait, the husband says, "Such a pity! They were so young, so full of promise."

"A bitter shame. Strangled in their beds while they slept, up those very stairs." The wife's friend nods toward the great hall. "First, the brother. Then the sister—they say she put up quite a struggle."

My ears ring so, I can't hear the rest. A cold shiver takes me.

Giles takes my elbow and leads me to the blazing yule log. "Let's warm ourselves, Sister."

I stretch out trembling hands, feel no warmth from the flames. I unclasp the pearl choker, and clutch it in my fist. A fist with five broken nails. And yet the ache round my throat is relentless.

SHARMON GAZAWAY's work has appeared or is forthcoming in The Forge Literary Magazine, MetaStellar, Daily Science Fiction, New Myths, Metaphorosis, Enchanted Conversation, Breath and Shadow, *and elsewhere. You can find her work in the anthologies,* Orpheus + Eurydice Rewoven, Wayward & Upward, Love Letters to Poe Volumes I and II, *and* Dark Waters. *Sharmon writes from the Deep South of the US where she lives beside a historic cemetery haunted by the wild cries of pileated woodpeckers. She is currently at work on a dark fantasy novel.*

The Shades of Midwinter

Andrew Lyall

Granny and I sat by the fire while Ma hovered at the window with her hot chocolate, surveying the darkness outside. This was our first Christmas since Ollie died and Dad left. We'd driven through the night, far up into the Highlands, to reach Granny before the snow arrived which cut off her village each year. Every room in our house felt empty now, and the journey north felt more like we were running away than travelling to be with family. Granny lanced more marshmallows and passed them to me to hold over the flames, but my mother's strange vigil kept snagging my attention.

"I don't see anything yet," Ma muttered without turning. I could see her wan reflection in the dark glass. She looked worried. I wanted her to be okay, but nothing would ever be okay again.

"What's she looking for?" I whispered. Granny tutted and shook her head. The lenses of her thick glasses were full of flames.

That morning we'd woken to a muffling blanket of white which seemed to deaden the air of the small valley. We'd gone outside and joined the rest of the villagers who were making snowmen, one for each of the twenty-three men, women and children who lived there. Even Granny. We had to wheel her out but she insisted on patting out a crooked, cold body and head as best she could with her bent, arthritic hands.

"Don't forget your token," she said as she puffed and strained, waving away any offer of help. Ma had explained the tradition on the way up, something she'd done each mid-winter as a little girl: you roll something personal into the body of your snowman, near the heart. Everyone in the village did it.

Now Ma kept watch over our effigies while Granny and I sat in the crackling orange circle of heat. Granny put a crooked finger to her lips and let me have a sip of her mulled wine while Ma was distracted. I pulled a face but took another sip when the mug was offered again.

Ma inhaled sharply and I snapped my head around. I was up and at her side before Granny could stop me. There were three shadowy figures on the lawn by our snowmen.

"Who are they?" I asked, but no one answered.

The fire popped.

As I cupped my face to the window I saw that there were more silhouettes standing outside other houses too. Each one was standing beside a snowman.

"Ma, what's going on?"

"I thought I'd imagined it," she murmured to herself, "all those years ago."

"Don't worry, petal," Granny said, "the shades don't bother us if we leave our tokens in our stead."

"You did leave a token didn't you?" Ma asked. Her expression frightened me.

"I thought," I stammered. "I thought Ollie should be here with us. I put his toy truck in my snowman." I didn't understand what was happening.

There was a light, dull knock at the door.

"Don't answer it!" Granny shouted.

A hollow, plaintive cry came from the other side.

"Ollie!" my mother called out and rushed to the door.

"Don't!"

Ma opened the door but her wide smile froze to something rictus as the cold charged in and filled the room.

ANDREW LYALL lives in the south of England where he hosts the YouTube channel Grumpy Andrew's Horror House. He has had stories published in the Horrortube anthologies Served Cold *and* Local Haunts, *and will soon be releasing his short story collection* 17 Stories of Death and Desire.

A Cardinal Sin

Lori Green

Sam stood up and took a break from digging, wiping the sweat from his furrowed brow. The night was cold and moonless, and he felt the inky darkness surround him, making it difficult to see. His fingers ached from the cold and the repeated strikes of his shovel against the frozen earth. He bent down and picked up the wooden box, warily lifting the lid. The cardinal laid there, stiff, its red feathers stained dark with blood. He looked up at the trees, shrouded in mist, and a shiver crawled its way down his spine. He had little time before sunrise.

The bird had fallen down the stovepipe earlier that night. He'd been out late and had come home in a drunken stupor before he could stoke the fire. Awakening sometime in the night, he found himself shivering on the floor, a soft tapping sound worming its way into his brain.

tap, tap, tap

Opening an eye, he noticed Ciana sitting on the bed, a ragged quilt thrown around her shoulders. She opened her mouth, but Sam held his forefinger against his lips, signaling for quiet.

tap, tap, tap

The sound echoed inside the stove. Frowning, Sam gripped the handle, slowly opening the door. He could see nothing until a flurry of flapping wings knocked him backwards. A cardinal flew aimlessly around the room until it spotted a window and flew towards it, hitting the glass hard. It dropped to the floor and laid there, still and lifeless, blood seeping into the floorboards. Ciana gasped, her hands clutching her swollen belly.

"You know what this means, Samuel. She knows." Her voice sounded hollow and flat. "We have to perform the protection ritual. Now. Before the solstice ends."

Sam looked at her. "Now?"

"Yes." Ciana hurried around the cabin, gathering her collection of dried herbs and fragrant oils along with a small bag of pebbles. "Here, take these." She shoved the items into Sam's arms and then scooped the dead bird up into her bare hands, placing it in a small wooden box, tucking its broken wing inside. "You'll have to go without

me. Burn it and bury it before first light." She looked up at him. "Otherwise, one of us will be dead by morning."

And so, he had come out to the woods to protect her, to bury their secret alone. He arranged the stones and watched as the feathers burned. Afterward he gathered the remains, placing the old box in the shallow grave and covering it with soil. He made his way back home, noticing a thin line of light on the horizon. It was done.

Sam's body ached with fatigue as he climbed under the blankets, his arm thrown protectively around his mistress. He fell into vivid dreams, until Ciana's screams rang in his ears and awakened him from slumber.

tap, tap, tap

She stood at the window, blood flowing freely down her legs. A cardinal perched there, shaking ash from its feathers like freshly fallen snow.

LORI GREEN *is a Canadian writer who has been writing poetry and dark fiction since she first picked up a pen. Her work has been accepted in various publications including Ghost Orchid Press, Dark Rose Press, Black Hare Press, and more. She studied English Literature at the University of Western Ontario and now lives along the shores of Lake Erie. She is currently working on her first novel. You can follow her on Twitter @LoriG1408 or on Facebook.*

Warm Hands, Cold Bones

April Yates

She wakes to pure white windows, as if during the night a cloud of confectioners' sugar from the bakery below has drifted up to coat them.

The scraping of her fingernail reveals it to be frost, the meagre fire having died overnight. The baker's son will already be downstairs laying the ovens fires ready for the day's work. It is days like this that make her glad for this small room and the job she'd been given. Her old bones wouldn't have survived another winter on the streets.

It hadn't always been that way. She remembers the days when the fire in the hearth was big enough to burn through the night. When a maid would fill the copper pan with hot sand to warm the sheets before bed. Although back then there was always someone else to cling to in the night. But society offers no validation for the love they had shared.

With her beloved's death came the turfing out onto the street. It was no wonder she went through the days like a ghost.

She dresses slowly—with every day that passes, each action seems to take a little more time than the day before—and goes downstairs.

She feels warmer here, but not by much. The cold has seeped deep into her, and it will not let go.

After dusting the counter with flour, blinding white against the dark wood, she turns away to collect the proofed dough. There in the flour's surface is a perfect handprint, delicate with long fingers. A woman's hand.

She lays her own beside it; it strikes a hauntingly familiar vision of hours sat side by side in blissful silence, a book in the other hand, knowing that the occasional smile was all that was needed.

She quickly smooths the flour, erasing the handprint. She can't succumb to dwelling on the past.

Throughout the day, the handprints keep appearing, impressed into soft dough, set in the flour and sugar. Once she could have sworn that she felt the phantom hand cup her cheek, imbruing blessed warmth into her skin.

Work complete for the day, she returns to her room, for where else could she go?

No friends or family on which to call upon.

The cold bites viciously at her, the room having not thawed during the day. Ice still clings thickly to the inside of the glass. She crawls, fully clothed, beneath the thin blankets, not bothering to lay a fire, and drifts into sleep.

It was the baker's son who discovered her early the next morning, sent up by his father when she failed to appear for work.

At first he thought her sleeping, though his own breath hung in the frigid air before him like plumes of smoke, and the air above her was clear.

Looking towards the window, he saw, etched into the frost, two handprints.

One slightly smaller than the other.

APRIL YATES is the author of the sapphic, historical horror-romance ASHTHORNE and other strange dark fictions. You can keep up to date with publications at aprilyates.com or find her spouting nonsense and posting inappropriate GIFs on Twitter @April_Yates

The Man Who Hated Christmas

Eleanor Sciolistein

I have heard it said, that there is no more curious beast upon the face of the Earth, than the man who hates Christmas.

Whilst I can to some extent understand this sentiment, I would counter that in certain extraordinary circumstances, such a hatred is somewhat understandable. Take, for example, my friend Clithers, who, when questioned about his odd aversion whilst sitting by the fireside one winter's eve, shared with me his reasons. Reasons which you may find, are quite convincing.

Clithers had, he said, been sitting in bed reading one night, when his attention was aroused by a strange sound. A small, subtle noise, he explained, that sounded for all the world,

"Like the faint, dappled tap of dirt, thrown by a mourner, onto a casket lid." Placing his book carefully down, Clithers sat up and listened. Again, the sound, from the corner, but this time, he thought, with an identifiable source. Soot, dislodged from within the chimney stack, disturbed no doubt by the wind that, even then, whistled loudly as it chewed past the brickwork.

Upon glancing toward the fireplace however, his eyes settled upon an unfamiliar shape.

At first, he was unable to make out quite what the curious object might be, but he felt certain not only that it was not a shape he had noticed before, but that it was something solid, protruding out from the bottom of the chimney.

Staring silently through the half-light, he resolved to make the short walk in stocking feet across the room. To carry the candle and investigate precisely what the shape might be. He did not, however, make it that far. For as he rose, creakily, from the bed, holding the candle before him, its pale, jaundiced glow threw a momentary flicker of light across the room and in turn, onto the object.

What he saw, was a head. Upside down and peeking out, so he said, from the bottom of the chimney. A face, grinning and inverted, which had, for who knew how long, simply been hanging there, silently in the dark, watching him as he read. A face, which, as he looked on in horror, licked its lips and smiled.

Clithers ran. He never stayed another night in that house and though it has remained uninhabited ever since, I have heard rumours. Whispers, about an odd shaped bottle filled with iron nails, hair and urine. A 'witch bottle' placed in the chimney breast as a charm against spirits and other dark things. A bottle which they say, 'should never have been removed'. Then, of course, there are the witnesses. Those who swear that they have seen smoke, formed in strange shapes and of the most hideous blackness, coming not 'out' from the chimney, but rather, 'going in'.

Since that night Clithers has refused to have any involvement with Christmas or the festivities surrounding it. "Something," he says, "about the way in which St Nicholas is said to enter the home," continues to make him uneasy.

ELEANOR SCIOLISTEIN is the pseudonym of Vincent Heselwood, a writer of gothic horror from Manchester, UK. Recently nominated for a 'Saturday Visiter Award' by The International Edgar Allan Poe Association, Vincent's collections of tales 'In the Style Of' *Poe and M.R. James, for Raventale Publishing, will be available in 2022.*

The Dead Come at Christmas

Maggie Nerz Iribarne

Polly was a pale girl with red hair who often thought about death. Her brother and sister and parents had died when she was very young. Her brother's body in his dark suit, the first she had ever seen, frightened and intrigued her. A few years later, Polly knelt beside her sister's casket, reached for her cool soft hand. Polly tried to picture what it would feel like for her own warm, familiar body to be stiff, cold. The solid fact of death followed her through her young life. She read the obituaries each week with an obsessive interest, constantly walked the cemetery, studying the names on the headstones.

At thirty, after she'd married Liam and had her children, she began seeing the dead people on Christmas Eve. There were hundreds of them, different ages and styles of dress, walking a candlelit road outside her house. That first time,

Polly stood at the window trembling, mouth agape. Of course, she was intrigued, but she was also terrified. She screamed for her son, Jarvis.

"What do you see?" she asked him, pointing out the window.

"Just darkness, Mommy."

From that point forward, she claimed that Christmas Eve made her sad, and everyone expected that Polly take to her bed for the holiday.

The years passed, Polly found herself to be an old woman with all of her family and friends dead. She did not know why she continued to live, why day after day her heart beat in her chest, her skin emanated warmth, her blood trickled through stiff veins.

Her ninety-fifth Christmas Eve, Polly got out of her bed, moved to the window, and saw the dead marching their solemn march. She stared at their faces, wanting desperately to recognize one of them. Liam? Jarvis? Beatrice? Mama? Papa? Her hand spread out on the cold window, hoping one of the spirit's own hands would mirror hers on the other side.

Polly took her walker, hobbled outside in her robe and slippers, the icy air clawing up her legs. For the first time in sixty-five years she walked out among her dreaded dead. They swirled, danced, swept around her, but it was not scary. Astounded by the silence, the lack of sadness, the warmth, she wanted to stay with them, always.

"Mrs. Cantwell!" her nurse, Cynthia, appeared, interrupted Polly's reverie, pulled her inside.

"What am I going to do with you?" she scolded. "Am I going to have to send you to the home?" Cynthia said, directing Polly inside to bed.

"You better be good, Mrs. C. No trouble." She touched Polly's cheek, shut off the light, closed and locked the door.

Polly, her blanket pulled up to her chin, listened to all the sounds, the ticking clock, the creaks and groans of the house. Her eyes moved to the end of the bed, where a collection of spirits assembled. A cloud-like finger reached out, beckoned her forward. Polly smiled, the joy of Christmas, at last, overwhelming her.

MAGGIE NERZ IRIBARNE is 52, living her writing dream in a yellow house in Syracuse, New York. She writes about teenagers, witches, the very old, bats, cats, priests/nuns, cleaning ladies, runaways, struggling teachers, and neighborhood ghosts, among many other things. She keeps a portfolio of her published work at https://www.maggienerziribarne.com.

House of Whispers

Warren Benedetto

The whispering woke me.

It was the girl, speaking in a low murmur. I didn't know her name, but I knew her voice. My wife and I had been hearing it since the day we moved in.

The house was a quaint Victorian built in the late 1800s by a local carpenter as a gift for his daughter. She passed it down to her daughter, who passed it down to her daughter, and so on up until today.

We knew from the moment we first entered that the place was perfect for us. We were made for it.

"Did you hear that?" I mumbled groggily.

There was no response. I rolled over to look at my wife. She was gone. I sat up and squinted into the darkness.

"Babe?" I called out.

Still no answer. I swung my feet down to the cold hardwood floor. It creaked as I stood.

"Babe?" I said again, a little louder this time. "You okay?"

An icy wind prickled my skin. Something brushed my shoulder. Out of the corner of my eye, I glimpsed a gauzy white apparition floating behind me. I spun around, then exhaled in relief. It was just a curtain blowing in through an open window. I brushed it away. *I closed this thing earlier*, I thought as I lowered the sash. *I know I did.*

That was one drawback of living in an old house: it seemed to have a life of its own. Lights turned on when you swore you had just turned them off. Doors and windows opened and closed, apparently of their own accord. Items went missing. Furniture moved by itself.

And every once in a while, my wife disappeared.

She wasn't usually gone for long. A few hours maybe. Then she'd reappear just as suddenly as she vanished, with no recollection of where she had been. All she could remember was the whispering. She couldn't understand what was being said, but it didn't seem dangerous. "It seemed sweet," she said. "Almost playful."

As I shuffled across the bedroom to look for my wife, my shin collided with something hard.

"God damn it!" I growled. A low wooden bench was toppled over in the middle of the room. I walked right into it.

"Did you move this?" I shouted to no one.

Suddenly, I felt a crushing tightness in my chest, as if a giant hand was closing around me. A nauseating wave of vertigo rolled my stomach. My body began to rise from the floor. I tried to fight off whatever was clutching me, but my arms were pinned to my side. I was completely immobilised.

I began to lose consciousness. As the world faded from grey to black, I heard the girl's voice in the darkness. It was louder now and clearer than ever before. For the first time, I could understand what she was saying.

"Tommy!" she shouted. "Give him back!"

"Why should I?" a boy's voice sneered.

"Because he's my doll, that's why!"

WARREN BENEDETTO writes short fiction about horrible people doing horrible things. He has a Master's degree in Film/TV Writing from USC. He is also the developer of StayFocusd, the world's most popular anti-procrastination app for writers. He built it while procrastinating. Visit www.warrenbenedetto.com and follow @warrenbenedetto on Twitter.

The Locked Door

Sally Hughes

It was a Christmas present from her friends, a night of pure luxury after a difficult year spent caring for her mum and missing Ali. A country-house hotel, all roaring fires and chilled cocktails, burnished copper and soft bathrobes.

At first Catherine felt awkward amongst the slender and beautiful people, but her bedroom amazed the anxiety out of her. To possess such a space for even a night was exhilarating. The most exquisite thing was, ridiculously, the communicating door. It was a deep treacle mahogany and carved with a long, sinuous bird, framed by flames of wood. A phoenix, emerging from its own exhausted remains vibrant and new. For some reason, Catherine tried the handle. It was locked by a large iron key that would have a twin on the other side.

Catherine met the man in the room next door as she went down to the spa. She greeted him shyly, embarrassed that he might have heard her rattling at their shared door. He gave a slow smile in response: tall and broad-shouldered, dressed in a crisp white shirt. A dusting of silver shone in his hair as though it had been touched by the frost outside.

She thought about him as the masseuse smoothed her tired, flabby body with long, loving strokes. She felt almost giddy, as if she were being beckoned into an unfamiliar country where she could remake herself. When she went down for dinner, he was again in the corridor. Catherine felt a warm tingle where his gaze rested on her neck, her ear-lobes.

Perhaps she was not so tired, not so flabby.

Kissing his mouth would be like drinking a glass of cool champagne.

Catherine could hear the soft sounds of his movements as she undressed for bed. Unzipping her skirt, she put her ear up against the communicating door, listening. When she traced the curving neck of the phoenix with her trembling finger, he paused. His breath drew near.

Only that locked door separated them.

Catherine heard the click of a bolt, and an exhalation of air. Slowly, she let her fingers slide down the phoenix and find the key. She turned it. The door jerked open.

He was waiting for her. He gave her the same slow smile, and opened his arms. Catherine stepped through the doorway, her blood thrumming with the thrill and terror of finally uncaging herself. Up close, there was a bluish tinge to the whites of his eyes. The elegant shirt had buttons of grey bone.

Too late, she realised what the unfamiliar country was.

He bent over her, his breath rank as a stagnant pond.

When they found her the next morning, in the empty room that was not her own, they could not understand how she had got there: sprawled on the plush carpet like a discarded dress, her hand reaching for the communicating door. It was locked on both sides.

SALLY HUGHES was brought up in West Yorkshire and lives in the West Highlands. She has a PhD in Scottish Literature and works as a Library Supervisor. Her stories have been published by Ghost Orchid Press, and she tweets at @sallyhbooks.

The Full Cold Moon

Alex Ebenstein

Ah, the Winter Solstice. Longest night of the year, when the season changes and the sun is reborn anew. It's a special one tonight, kids, what with the full moon. The 'full cold moon', the old farmers call it. Which, with a fresh blanket of snow, I suppose makes this the longest *and* the brightest night. I was but a young girl the last time it happened, sitting 'round this very hearth, though it was *my* Gramma spinning yarns about the myths and mysteries of the Solstice. That night she shared a legend I'll never forget, about the ghosts released from their ethereal prisons, free to roam the earth for one night, sundown to sunup.

Why are they free to roam, you ask? Well, certainly you must know ghosts are roused on nights of cosmic significance—your eclipses and solstices and such. Though normally they're held back by the places they haunt, say, the walls of an old Victorian or the gates of the town cemetery. Your great-great grandmother didn't know why the full cold moon granted them a special reprieve, but that's what they get. They're able to move beyond their normal spectral boundaries, chasing any whim or weary so long as they return home before sunrise.

Where and why do they go? Who and what do they see? Lord only knows. Most are harmless, of course, like your everyday human. But, naturally, there are some who left this world angry, made angrier still from their perpetual confinement in a wraithlike state on earth. Gramma had a theory these mean ones did more than roam. They take a vengeance, they do, searching for a new home to haunt or person to possess.

Oh, don't you pay that noise any mind, it's only the wind tickling the eaves.

Is it true? Can they overtake a home or, God forbid, a person? I suppose I don't know for sure, but I tell you, children, I haven't tried to find out. My Gramma claimed to have seen a vengeful spirit when she was a young lass. Felt its chill before she saw it, colder than the winter air. A dingy gray form gliding across the blindingly white landscape, teeth bared and smeared a scarlet hue. It chased her down on the way to the outhouse, it did, but she ran like the devil back inside, safe again before the ghost could attack.

They're free to roam, mind you, but are forbidden from entering homes of the living, unless invited.

What's that? Of course I feel the chill drifting through here. It's nothing but the result of the fire burning low.

Now, what was I saying? Ah, yes, the ghosts … I never did see one that night, the last full cold moon. Then again, I never ventured outside to tempt fate …

Well, run along now, children. Fetch some wood from the shed for your Gramma to keep this fire burning. And watch each other's backs in the moonlight, lest the ghosts get you.

ALEX EBENSTEIN is a maker of maps by day, writer of horror fiction by night. He lives with his family in Michigan. He has stories published by The Other Stories Podcast, Cemetery Gates Media, and others. He is also the founder of Dread Stone Press. Find him on Twitter @AlexEbenstein.

Dreadful Things

Nicole Little

The hearth is cold as ice; no welcoming fire burns within. Likewise, the lamp sits extinguished on the side table; no candles glow upon the tree. It is a blessed Christmas Eve, yet I sit in pitch darkness, a shawl clasped tightly at my neck, gossamer lace twisted between my knuckles.

There is no merriment in this house.

On this of all nights.

I suppress a shiver that has little to do with the chill of the parlour as the clock ticks ever closer to midnight. My fingers twitch at the heavy draperies as I wait, and wait, and wonder. Will they will return as they have done years past, those specters at my window?

Lavender House is both my refuge and my prison as Christmas looms. My mind wanders back to my youth when balsam fir and pipe smoke perfumed the halls this time of year. Evenings when father would sit near the fire, bowl of Smoking Bishop at his elbow, as he read the story of the Christ child, born in a manger. And mother, preparing the evening feast, in a kitchen resplendent with the scent of roasting goose.

But father and mother are long gone. I am left to carry this burden alone.

A rap comes at the window. Then, the screech of nails across the thick frost that coats the pane. I fall back against the wall; fearful they may see me. Hand pressed against my mouth; I hold back a scream that threatens release. Though I have been expecting them, terror numbs me to my core. My shawl slips to the floor.

A ghost of a whisper now, beside my ear. I strain to hear; faint though it is, perhaps I may glean from it just why they return each year to torment me so.

Something slams into the wall at my back.

Is that laughter?

Another thud. I hear the glass in the window crack.

All at once, I am incensed. Enough of this.

I cannot recall moving yet here I am, in front of the great mahogany door. I cast it open and roar: “Away from my home you foul beasts! Leave me in peace!”

Three tall figures scatter towards the murky copse of trees beyond the manor, screaming words that have no meaning to me: *It's her! It's her! I told you it was true!*

I return to the parlour and retrieve my shawl from the floor, draping it back 'round my shoulders as the door creaks shut on the dreadful things that lurk beyond the light.

NICOLE LITTLE lives in Newfoundland, Canada. Her short stories have appeared in seventeen anthologies. Her first novella, The Lotus Fountain: A Slipstreamers Adventure *launched November 2020. In her spare time, Nicole has either a pen in her hand or her nose in a book. She is married with two daughters.*

Bone Kindling

Sophia DeSensi

Fat. So very fat. Each hairy finger protrudes his bed of thatch. Greasy hands loll across the hearth. I jam his limbs within the blaze and plop the cauldron atop his swollen gut. I should have shaved him. Bald and naked, he'd meet his tomb.

I yank our silver band, tugging it over each worm-like wrinkle, each pugged knot of his finger. I twiddle the ring between my coffin nails. "Does the gap feel familiar?"

"Frr—ee—cho," he moans with threaded lips. Speckles of holly berry juice drool down the nape of his neck, sweet enough to suck.

"Psycho?" I've been called worse. In comparison, it's barely a curse. At least, this time it's more accurate than his previous slander: spoiled, bitch, gold digger. As if I'd dirty myself. No, when these hands greet soil, it'll be to dig his grave.

A breeze whistles through the chimney, carrying flakes of frost and scents of evergreen.

He squirms, jostling the pot.

"Uncomfortable?" I kick his side.

His toes scratch the quarry tiles. I don't know what he expects to accomplish. He's not a mole. He can't burrow himself out. Not this time.

I jab a birch log beneath his back, splitting flesh. He rolls to the side. Flames lick lashes.

Tears—tears I've yearned so very long for finally surmise. Blood vessels bulge and crimson milk oozes across his stubble. Thrashing and gurgling, he scrapes the hearth.

"Stop it," I say. "You're making me sick."

I drop our ring and brandy splashes. Thick like syrup, it drips along his round-jaw and seeps through splintered wood.

I flit a match and guide it to shreds of burlap stuffed between his pits. The brindles catch flame, and I blow, blow, blow. Hot plumes flicker. Slink across his shirt. Sizzle atop cotton. Skin like parchment sloughs from his cuticles and peel from his bone. I gag, caressing my nose to my sleeve. But peek. I must peek.

Bubbles of cinnamon and cider burst and steam. I stir the brandy and wine. Luscious berries and cloves drift to the surface. I'll drink my closure like Marie Laveau. A toast to our life no longer à deux.

He moans and groans and whines his last lament.

"Hush," I say. "I can't hear the mulled wine simmer."

SOPHIA DESENSI earned a Bachelor's in creative writing with a minor degree in medical anthropology and a Master of Fine Arts in writing popular fiction from Seton Hill University. As a graduate student, she apprenticed under New York Times and USA Today best-selling authors, such as Maria V. Snyder, Priscilla Oliveras, and Lee McClain. She currently works as an editor at the Parliament House Press and is the author of the award-winning short fiction, "Tiny Hearts" in the anthology, Dragons of a Different Tail.

Two of her YA fantasy novels were critiqued by NYT and USA Today best-selling author, Maria V. Snyder. For a year and a half, she workshopped her YA fantasy thesis novel under the mentorship of Kathryn Miller Haines (award winning playwright and author of YA novels for HarperCollins and Simon & Schuster). She furthered her education with developmental editing courses at the Editorial Freelancers Association and is a member of SCBWI, EFA, and APSS.

Die Kleine Weihnachtmaus

J. L. Royce

The family settled by the Christmas Tree—Father and Mother and grown children: oldest daughter flush with life growing within her, son eager to retreat to bed with his lover, two teenagers impatient to commune with friends. And Nana.

Gaunt amidst plenty, solemn surrounded by mirth, succinct when offered conversation, Nana was unaffected by the plenty around her. So all were surprised when she straightened in her chair, cleared her throat, and spoke.

"It was a night like this …" she began, "… far away …"

A little girl lay in her dormered bedroom, impatient for Christmas morning. She heard the front door open and voices below, and crept out to the top of the narrow staircase. She peered down, shivering, to watch the officer stroll about the sitting room.

He was tall and handsome, and with his leather duster open resembled a great black crow, wings rustling. Mother held a tray of cookies, Father, a glass of *schnapps*; so this, she thought, must be a friend. The man looked directly at the girl and smiled.

Ah, a Christmas Mouse! he said. Mother rushed to intercept, apologizing, but the officer beckoned the girl down. *Come, have a biscuit with me*. She slowly descended, wary of the tension in her parents' eyes.

I'm trying to find some friends. He offered her the plate. *They're playing hide-and-seek*. He dropped to one knee, elegantly as a prince in a storybook. *Have you seen anyone hiding, little mouse?*

She shook her head and her parents relaxed. Then she said, *I hear mice, Mother says, but they whisper. I do not know the words*.

He glanced at the soldier by the door. *Where?* he asked, eyes gleaming, and she pointed up, over the fireplace: next door.

The officer murmured; the soldier saluted and departed.

It's cold; let's watch from here. He beckoned her to the window.

She stepped reluctantly over, accepting another cookie. He opened the curtains and then his gloved hands fell heavily upon her thin shoulders: *So you'll remember*.

The soldier's squad entered next door, and in minutes the street filled with strangers, shivering in bedclothes, some without shoes.

Ah, said the officer.

Someone ran and was shot; then more guns rose, and shouted, until the snow ran red.

The officer glanced at her parents, then bent close to the girl. *So you'll always remember, not to lie.*

The little girl grew to become a fine woman: prosperous, with a kind husband and healthy children, with everything she wanted before that night. Yet always she felt the officer's heavy hands, not her lover's caresses, she tasted the cookies, she heard the rifles, she saw the blood—none of the goodness. She confessed to priests; finally, one said, *You must tell the world your truth.*

Nana fell quiet. Father rose, fussed with the fire to dispel the uneasy darkness in the room. When he looked up, Nana was smiling, eyes closed.

"Time for bed, Mother," he said. But when he kissed her cheek it was already cold.

J. L. ROYCE is a published author of science fiction, the macabre, and whatever else strikes him. He lives in the northern reaches of the American Midwest, exploring the wilderness without and within. His work appears in Allegory, Fifth Di, Fireside, Ghostlight, Love Letters to Poe, Lovecraftiana, Mysterion, parABnormal, Sci Phi, Strange Aeon, Utopia, Wyldblood, *etc. He is a member of HWA and GLAHW. Some of his anthologized stories may be found at: www.jlroyce.com. Twitter: @authorJLRoyce.*

Escher's Tree House

SJ Townend

Douglas felt apathetic about his tree house, yet—even in the midst of winter—he visited it every day. A stone's throw from his bedroom window, just hidden from the prying eyes of his folks, he whiled away many an hour there with friends.

But it wasn't really a tree house, more an area of leaves, mossy sticks, and animal bones, arranged into an oval on the snow-covered ground. He'd meet there regularly with his chums, who'd all sworn allegiance to each other, to have each other's backs, who'd formed an unshakeable gang. Despite this pact of loyalty, Douglas still felt blasé about the arrangement.

They weren't so much a gang anyhow—or even really friends. More a collection of soft toys he'd had since he was tiny. Some felt gloppy, others smelt funny—of rot and age—and many had worn patches on their bottoms.

Douglas loved to run and skip and jump, except he didn't. He just sat in the same spot in his house of bones and decay and rocked back and forth in time with the breeze that blew the snow.

And the snow was a polymer of sorts, made from time glued to tears.

Douglas hugged his teddies whilst sat in his spot because he figured that's what young boys were supposed to do, but he didn't feel much love for his toys. And they weren't really teddies at all, but the sticks and leaves and animal bones which he'd fashioned into rough shapes to represent living things. Or what he'd imagined living things to be shaped like. The largest one was shaped like a woman.

Douglas had been raised by his beautiful mother. He'd looked at her through dilated pupils brimming with adoration, oxytocin. Except he hadn't really looked at her in any way at all—his eyes had worn away to dents. And his mother was not his mother, but an old hag witch who'd snatched him from his birth parents when he was five days old, whilst his true mother had slept beside him, whilst he'd babbled by and with the river.

And it hadn't been an actual river, or even a stream. It'd been a strip of silver-foiled paper that'd meandered in stationary two-dimension from one side of his estate to the other, in front of his glass castle which he resided in—

—which wasn't a glass castle at all.

There were no crystal turrets, no drawbridge of ice, and he didn't really like existing within the realm of his estate either, as it was in fact a snow globe sat upon the top shelf of a child's bookcase in which the boy was trapped inside … in which the old crone who spoke in cobwebs had exiled him to on discovering he was one for telling porkies.

Dusty, hidden, and untouched, the domed paperweight remained shelved, in a room kitted out for a baby who'd been snatched, whose mother had never had the heart to empty out.

SJ TOWNEND has been writing ~~evil lies~~ dark fiction in Bristol for three years. She's currently putting together a collection of horror stories, working title: SICK GIRL SCREAMS. *SJ hopes her stories take the reader on a journey to often a dark place and only sometimes back again. Find her on Twitter @SJTownend.*

Do You See What I See?

Jessica McHugh

She died alone, in a house full of people.

While music and laughter swelled like cigar smoke in the other rooms of the Blackwood home, Marie's room was silent. Even the snow on her empty window-box fell louder than her final breath, and she was glad of it. Snow had such a short time to tell its story, and she'd had plenty. She'd lived as an ornament, glittering like a snowflake in frozen lace, and it hadn't served her well.

The time had come to melt.

The annual Blackwood Christmas party stretched on with no one wondering what became of Marie. And why would they? She'd baked cookies and hung stockings. She'd set out the gilded crystal punch bowl. What else could she do but fade into the background? The kids rarely thought of anyone but themselves, and Jerome was only attentive when he had something to hide, which he usually did.

With cocktails fueling the festivities, the family's blind spots bled through them like the feathered ink on a blank check. That's where Marie hid to make her preparations.

She wasn't hasty. In the weeks before the party she waved red flags like a matador, inviting someone to change her mind. But her efforts went largely unnoticed. Jerome thanked her for the lack of "gift debris" that year, but didn't connect the lack of debris to the lack of gifts. The kids expressed gratitude that she wasn't nagging them about watering the Christmas tree, but no one noticed it was dead by the morning of the party.

Brown needles littered the tree skirt, which was just one piece of holiday decor she used to cover the tubes running from the gas-guzzling beasts in the garage and throughout the Blackwood home. Tinsel, Marie discovered, hid a multitude of sins.

Alcohol too. Though she didn't drink that day, the Blackwoods would blame the cocktails for every blush and dizzy spell, if only to explain their own. Though spirits were involved, the pinholes in the tubing were harder at work as Marie woozily made her way to the bedroom. To the drowsy end, the family remained blissfully ignorant—to her plan, her death, and to the first three Mrs. Blackwoods watching them choke on air.

The title of "Mrs. Blackwood" was ephemeral as snow—and just as burdened by beauty that dazzled and warmed and unmade itself within a season. And like snow, what they left behind was drastically different from what they'd been at their peaks. Something once so lovely and unique became filthy slush. More curse than memory, more stain than ghost.

The Blackwood home was rife with stains Jerome and the kids were too conceited to see in life—and it followed them into death. They couldn't see the police who discovered their bodies two days later, nor the former matriarchs that conspired against them. They couldn't even see each other as they walked from room to room.

They'd woken alone, in a house full of people … and they would never know.

JESSICA McHUGH is a 2x Bram Stoker Award-nominated poet, a novelist, & an internationally-produced playwright running amok in the fields of horror, sci-fi, young adult, and wherever else her peculiar mind leads. She's had twenty-five books published in thirteen years, including her bizarro romp, The Green Kangaroos, *her YA series,* The Darla Decker Diaries, *and her Elgin Award nominated blackout poetry collections,* A Complex Accident of Life *and* Strange Nests.

Instagram: theJessMcHugh
Twitter: theJessMcHugh
www.McHughniverse.com

The Man of the House

Rebecca Jones-Howe

Jack woke to the shadow again. It stood in the kitchen and drifted slowly, its limbs hanging motionless as though the figure was wary of the space that it occupied. The floors creaked beneath it. A cupboard door rattled before it. Goosebumps prickled Jack's flesh but he didn't dare move. The shadow always vanished if he did, and so he feigned sleep, his body taut with apprehension. He held his breath and thought of death again.

The pondering of death always came so naturally now. Dread had followed Jack since the Great Crash, from which he'd escaped with only a hastily-packed suitcase and a gun. He'd traveled from his New York brownstone to a run-down bachelor suite in Baltimore, hoping his many debts and obligations wouldn't follow. He kept his clothes in the suitcase and the gun beneath his mattress. The cold metal always chilled him at night, even when the apartment's radiator ticked its endless metronome against winter's fury outside. Jack tried not to rely upon the radiator too much, though he had no choice but to keep it running through the recent snap of cold. It ticked rapidly, always giving Jack the feeling that he wasn't the only one relying on the heat it supplied.

The shadow rummaged slowly through the kitchen, but it wasn't the only apparition that plagued Jack. Soon enough, the pipes in the bathroom emitted their angry groans again. Jack felt them now, like fists gripping around his heart. They'd first came from the shower, activated whenever Jack returned from work. He'd wash away the day's filth, but something always lingered at his feet, laying in the tub beneath him. Something sad. Something wrong.

The restless pipes now encompassed the apartment, hammering through the walls in an enraged embrace. In the kitchen, the small shadow whimpered. Jack emitted a gasp, for this was first time the specter made a noise. It looked weary and its voice sounded tinny and distant, accompanying the throbbing pipes in the walls. Jack shifted in the bed, only for the shadow to flinch in response.

"Papa?"

The pipes groaned louder, provoking Jack to finally respond. He scrambled for the gun. Tears burned behind his eyes and he blinked them free, his face red with shame as he pointed the gun at the shadow. The pipes banged, shaking the very walls behind him.

"Some men came and took Mommy in the bathroom, Papa. Now she won't wake up."

Debt. Dread. Death.

"The men kept saying your name, Papa."

He tried to exhale but the ache in his chest swelled now that he'd been found.

"I'm so hungry, Papa."

The shadow moved toward him. Its haze of darkness reached with long skinny arms. Jack scrambled out of bed, only to lose his balance. He tried to catch himself, only for the heat of the radiator to burn his palm. He slipped to the floor in pain, moaning as the burn worked through his hand like a final lash for his betrayal. The heater ticked. The pipes wailed.

"We need you, Papa."

Jack pressed the gun's kiss to his temple, finally ready to apologize.

REBECCA JONES-HOWE lives in Kamloops, British Columbia. Her work can be found in PANK, Dark Moon Digest, *and* The New Black: A Neo-Noir Anthology, *among many others. Her first collection of short fiction, Vile Men, was published in 2015. She is a regular contributor for* The Crow's Quill Magazine. *Find her at rebecca-joneshowe.com.*

A Victorian Secret

Jay Seate

Harold Bartholomew's Victorian parlor was aglow with a soft light reflecting off tree ornaments. Gold and silver presents gleamed, but Elizabeth was the most splendid jewel of all. She stood waiting with strands of tinsel in her hair, as requested.

"Merry Christmas, darling," he said.

His housekeeper had left early. It would be only he and Elizabeth, and her sweet smile. As Harold gazed into her eyes, his pulse quickened. Prayerfully, he whispered, "You have given me such sweet memories. Tonight, I am yours and you are mine."

Harold carried Elizabeth to the Persian rug in front of the glowing fireplace Josephine had tended until she departed.

"Do you remember the night," Harold said, "in the carriage? How distracted I was from overindulgence. We rushed home to make love. Can you ever forgive me?"

"Yesss," he thought she sighed.

Elizabeth made musical sounds like the air blown through the mouthpiece of a fipple-flute. In each other's arms, there existed a delusion of safety from the world beyond this cozy parlor.

"Let's continue to begin every Christmas this way," Harold breathed. "Just like this, till the end of time."

On Christmas Day, Josephine let herself into her employer's home with her passkey. Her eyebrows rose at the sight of Mr. Bartholomew on the floor in front of a cold hearth, the second Christmas she had found him in such a state. She blushed at his nakedness, but could not deny a certain thrill. An empty decanter of whiskey lay nearby.

"Didn't eat a thing. Just drank your dinner, I'll wager. But who could blame you, you pathetic man, considering the terrible carriage accident. Two years ago last night it was." *If it could only be me next to you instead of those two-year-old, unopened packages ... and this creature.*

Josephine chastised herself for her lascivious feelings, but it was Christmas. She noticed a sprig of mistletoe clutched in Bartholomew's fist. *Had I been under the mistletoe, might he have given me a kiss?*

"When I come next week, I'm going to wear a bright frock instead of these old cleaning rags and maybe you'll come out of your fantasies and take notice of me."

Josephine picked up the humanlike, mechanical doll with the lifelike face her employer had created. The clockwork mechanism activating her music box had long since run down, but the eyes opened slowly, the counterbalanced lids of a doll's eyes, which caused Josephine to shiver.

The heart oftentimes rules the head, a recipe for either joy or disaster. Josephine placed the copy of Harold's dead wife, an affront to all that was decent, she believed, back in the closet and slipped out of the house, leaving her employer with his dreams and liquor-induced slumber.

The parlor was quiet now. Harold could feel the memory of Elizabeth's ghostly touch engraved on his skin. He heard carolers singing, *God Rest ye Merry Gentlemen.* His lips moved slowly. "Thank you, Elizabeth. Until next Christmas Eve, my darling. Happy New Year."

JAY SEATE stands on the side of the literary highway and thumbs down whatever genre comes roaring by. His storytelling runs the gamut from Horror Novel Review's Best Short Fiction *to the* Chicken Soup for the Soul *series. His fiction incorporates fantasy, suspense, or humor featuring the quirkiest of characters.*

Some Ghosts are Made

Vivian Kasley

It was Christmas when you called. I should've known you would, it was our most treasured holiday together. You'd drank an entire bottle of wine during dinner and after everyone left, you slumped to the floor and shouted my name, "William!" Your voice echoed around my soul like bubbles rippling around skin in water. I was minding my own business, finding my way in the unknown and then you summoned and tugged me back with such force, that if I still had lungs, they would've burst. I was trying hard to forget and almost had, and then I was a ghost, barely there, but there enough.

When I could focus, I saw you. Your merlot-stained lips and teeth, and the bit of gravy you'd splashed onto your green blouse. Your hair was in a bun, tendrils hung around your delicate oval face, which was wet from crying. And still, you were devastatingly beautiful. I wanted to touch you, but couldn't. The unbearable anguish of that was too much, so I floated into the family room, where you'd half-heartedly set up a tree. You tried Elizabeth; I could tell. If I could've cried, I would've, but ghosts don't have that ability. All we can do is watch, and want, and feel like we're dying all over again.

You fell asleep with your face pressed to the cold tile, and for hours I watched. I know it was your first Christmas without me, and I probably would've done the same if you'd left me first. But I wish I could tell you, not all ghosts want to be ghosts. Some are made by those who can't let go, we're tethered to our callers. We suffer alone, hearing you barter for our return when you think you're in an empty room. That's the worst part.

Morning came, and you woke, confused about you where you were, but then you remembered. You yawned and rose slowly, stretching your back. The dishes were still in the sink, so you began to wash them, tears joining the soapy water below. You picked up the carving knife, the good one we'd picked out together. There were still bits of turkey stuck to it, so you wiped them away with your hand, cutting it open in the process. You hissed in pain, and blood ran down your arm in a stream. As soon as your mouth quivered, I knew. You wailed, then held the knife against your throat. I screamed into the void, I screamed loud enough to shatter space and time, but no one heard me.

I was plunged back between worlds. As before, my form was searching for a place to rest. Though I willed myself to stop, I couldn't. I wanted to wait and see if you'd show. Where were you? But then I realized, someone must've called you back. I had to keep moving, Elizabeth, I hope you'll understand. After all, who knew how long it'd be before they let you go.

VIVIAN KASLEY hails from the land of the strange and unusual, Florida! She's a writer of short stories and poetry which have appeared in various science fiction anthologies, horror anthologies, horror magazines, and webzines. Some of her street cred includes Ghost Orchid Press, Diabolica Americana, *The Denver Horror Collective's* Jewish Book of Horror, *Kandisha Press's* Slash-Her, *and poetry in Black Spot Books inaugural women in horror poetry showcase:* Under Her Skin. *She's got more upcoming, including a tale in Grimscribe Press's* Vastarien. *When not writing or subbing at the local middle school, she spends her time reading in bubble baths, snuggling her rescue cats and dogs, going on foodie dates with her other half, and searching for seashells and other treasures along the beach.*

1.https://www.facebook.com/bizarrebabewhowrites/

2. amazon.com/author/viviankasley

3. https://twitter.com/VKasley

The Deserter

Anthony Engebretson

The trees gazed down at him like owls watching a helpless mouse. The cold stung his skin, at least wherever he could still feel, and snow spat disdainfully into his eyes. But he kept trudging forward. If he stopped to rest, he would surely die. He prayed for an end to this forest, cursing the day he was sent to this wretched island. He yearned for home, to feel the warm kiss of the Mediterranean against his face.

But there was no going home. He was a deserter, having abandoned his post for a life with Juliana. But now she was gone, their village was gone, decimated by Saxon raiders. Worse yet, there would be no retribution. The empire was no longer in this land. Perhaps there was no empire anywhere. What was truly left of home, torn asunder by civil strife and barbarians?

A faint noise whispered through the bitter wind—a distant echo of drums. His heart tightened. Saxons? Despite the pain and despair, he was not ready to join his love. With the feeble energy he had left, he quickened his pace. But far as he went, the eerie drumbeats followed, never coming closer yet never fading from his ears.

He halted when he saw a figure standing among the trees. It was a man, gaunt and pale, sunken eyes staring at the deserter. He didn't look like a Saxon, but he was a warrior. Blue paint streaked his pallid skin and gold rings adorned his arms. He was unarmed: no weapon, no shield.

The deserter blinked snow from his eyes, and when he looked again, a woman was suddenly standing beside the warrior. She was also pale and unarmed, her long red hair frayed. Yet she stood proudly, her eyes stabbing the deserter with fiery hatred. His soul constricted when he realized that, behind the two watchers, were hundreds of faded figures, ashen faces from youthful to withered, hovering among the trees. All looked only at him.

The ghostly drumbeats continued, neither growing louder nor softening. The deserter resumed walking, as quickly as his frozen body allowed. None of the figures moved. Had they surged for him, he would be at their mercy. But they only watched, hundreds of hollow eyes observing a pathetic man in a place he didn't belong. He did not deign to meet their eyes; he just kept stumbling forward until, through the blinding air, a Roman villa appeared in the distance. Its glow was faint, as if on the verge of fading for good. But it was there, and he praised God.

As he came closer to the villa, the drumbeats finally faded. He no longer felt empty eyes watching him. Only one last sound echoed through the air: the ghostly trill of war cries, winding victoriously through the trees. As quickly as the sound erupted, it ceased, as if it had been a trick of the wind.

ANTHONY ENGEBRETSON is a dark speculative fiction writer living in Lincoln, Nebraska. He has been published in several anthologies and his debut novella will be published by Ghost Orchid Press in 2022.
Twitter: @AnthonyJEngebr1
Blog: https://raccoonalleyblog.wordpress.com/

Spirit of the Seasons

Marisca Pichette

There's a package under the tree I can never open.

It's been there every year, as far back as I can remember. I didn't buy it. I didn't wrap it. I didn't put it under the tree.

December 24, it arrives. December 26, it leaves.

The paper changes, but the shape doesn't. One year it was wrapped in snowflakes, another in candy canes. Once, reindeer with cartoon smiles. Once, plain brown paper and string, like a bomb.

I know it when I touch it, lift it up. It weighs too little. Less than an empty box should weigh. Less than the paper that covers it.

Nothing worth anything could weigh so little, take up so little space.

This morning I feel it arrive. Christmas Eve, like always. Coffee in hand, I walk into the dining room. The tree stands in the corner, shedding needles on the hardwood floor.

Where nothing should be, there's a small box. This year it's wrapped in silver. Glitter dusts the floor around it.

I haven't touched it in years. I know what it says on the label. I should leave it where it is, wait until it goes again.

I used to have to dig to find the box with its folded label, the message inside burned into my memory better than any face. Now, it's the only gift I get.

On my mantle, I have only one Christmas card.

Standing across from the tree, I'm tempted to open the box. In my family, we had a tradition. One present could be opened on Christmas Eve.

One.

I set my coffee down, palms sweating. Will it work this year? I kneel in front of the tree and drag my only present across the floor, leaving a trail of glitter and needles. I'll never get another gift. No one's left to remember me.

Fingers shaking, I bend the label back, reading a note written in blood.

My blood. My handwriting.

Take me back. Eternity isn't worth this.

I fold the note closed. The paper has no edge, no weakness. I tried cutting it, smashing the box flat. Light as it is, it never tears, never gives in to me. I push the box away. It weighs almost nothing, my soul.

On the mantle, my only Christmas card stands alone. I stop and pick it up. Even this weighs more, feels more real than the box under the tree.

Inside is a note written in gold pen.

Have a wonderful year!

The message hasn't changed once, in a century of cards. I touch his signature and try to remember my name. I didn't think to write it on the note after he wrapped me up and promised to grant my Christmas wish.

In the light of the tree, his words shimmer like flames.

With love,

Lucifer.

MARISCA PICHETTE is an author of speculative fiction, nonfiction, and poetry. More of her work can be found in Strange Horizons, Pseu-doPod, Apparition Lit, Fireside Magazine, *and* PodCastle, *among oth-ers. Her speculative poetry collection,* Rivers in Your Skin, Sirens in Your Hair, *is forthcoming in Spring 2023 with Android Press.*

Mr Swill's Generosity

Scotty Sarafian

For three days, Clifford had watched mourners, rich and poor, flock to the grave of Mr. Gregory Swill. Their grief had marked the mound, its surface having become mottled from those who had knelt in prayer.

Swill had been regarded in life as a man of divine generosity.

Few wealthy individuals could travel the slums safely, but he had wandered unmolested; after all, a significant portion of Whitechapel's thieves and pickpockets had been fed by his charity.

Clifford's employment had afforded him just one sighting of the beloved figure whose walks had coincided with his contractual hours. On that particular morning, the gentleman, in deviation from his typical route, had hobbled past the docks, a black cane guiding his every step. Indeed, he had appeared slender, as though every morsel of food passed to those beneath him.

With Christmas soon approaching, Clifford had decided to adapt to present circumstances in order to pursue Swill's donation. Having considered local reverence, he had selected Clerkenwell men, Quick and Barker, to help him plunder the corpse; they had been unfamiliar with the deceased and, thus, had readily accepted the proposition.

Carolers' voices permeated the cemetery wall. Their song, audible from the pit where he and Barker stood, was Sarah's favorite, about a king named Wenceslas. Clifford pictured his daughter, her eyes twinkling upon the rocking horse in Rutherford's shop window.

Barker pried open the coffin lid without hesitation. He recoiled at the stench, backing into Clifford, who managed to maintain his balance.

"Hurry, will yer?" Quick hissed from his lookout above.

Clifford handed Barker the lantern, skirted him, and neared the body.

A wool overcoat swaddled the emaciated being whose odor had infected its every thread. Sinewy hands, folded to his chest, sheathed the crook of an ebony cane.

Averting his gaze from the ghastly face, Clifford slid a ring from Swill's finger. He unraveled the silk tie next, stuffed it inside his trousers' pocket, then plucked the cufflinks from the sleeves before promptly closing the lid.

He exchanged his share of the pawned returns for Rutherford's rocking horse on the ensuing day. When Clifford returned home that evening, Rebecca stole a single glance at the object and continued stirring the lentils.

"Already asleep," said his wife.

Clifford deposited the present in their bedroom, whereupon he visited Sarah in hers and, quietly, brought the blanket upon her shoulders. Surely, he thought, Swill would have understood.

The rocking horse began to creak from across the house.

Clifford emerged, closing the door behind him so that his daughter would not hear. Rebecca was at the hob, her position unchanged. Perplexed, he paced into their room.

The figure was hunched behind the gift, a vulpine smile sprawled across his sunken face. Missing from his burial garments were the pilfered pieces. He lifted his cane and struck the horse's nuzzle once, then twice. Flames swallowed the creature on the third hit. As its wood collapsed, grey plumes shrouded the gentleman whose generosity had, undeniably, reached its threshold.

Originally from Boca Raton, Florida, SCOTTY SARAFIAN grew up in Dublin, Ireland and Wilmington, Delaware. He graduated from Rollins College with a bachelor's in English; he is a graduate of Trinity College Dublin's M. Phil program in popular literature. Scotty's most recent work has appeared in Coffin Bell, Black Hare Press, *and* Pulp Modern Flash. *Upcoming publications:* Black Hare Press: Year 4, Opulent Syntax: Irish Speculative Fiction. *He lives in Dublin, Ireland.*

The Boy in the Lake

Alice Austin

Eddie Fowler went missing last Christmas. His body was never found.

They say he probably walked across a frozen lake and the ice broke beneath him. The cold snatched his breath away in an instant, icy fingers clenching his heart, piercing straight through to his bones. He instantly went into shock, unable to climb out. The ice sealed itself above him as he sank to his grave.

Steve was thinking about Eddie as he ran, following his sister's footprints in the snow. His chest burned as he gasped out clouds of steam into the freezing air.

Lisa and Eddie had been friends, but she hadn't been upset when he disappeared. They'd assumed she was too young to understand that her friend was gone for good, but now Steve knew they'd got it wrong. Eddie wasn't gone.

The snow pelted him as he ran, tiny flakes attacking his exposed skin with icy nips.

Eddie's body lay lost in a lake, but his spirit roamed freely through water. Eddie was in the rain and in the snow. Eddie was in the morning frost that covered the grass and the icicles hanging from the roof. Steve had only realised what was happening when he saw Lisa talking to a puddle. When he went to look, he saw a rippled reflection that belonged to neither of them.

Steve could see Eddie watching him, refracted eyes peering out from the icicles that hung from the trees. Tendrils of fog curled around the floor. Misty hands reached up to grab his arm, but they couldn't hold him.

Steve gasped as he saw Lisa up ahead, dressed up in her puffy red coat and scarf.

"Lisa!" he shouted, running forwards. Terror shot through his veins as the ground creaked beneath him. He lifted a foot and saw ice, hidden by a thin coating of snow. He held out his arms. "Lisa, come back. Quickly."

She turned to face him and grinned, oblivious to the danger.

"Steve! I've found Eddie. He's happy to see us. He's been alone for a whole year." Steve looked to her feet. Eddie Fowler's corpse stared up at his sister, pressing a pale hand against the underside of the ice.

"Don't be scared," Lisa said, smiling and crouching down to press her hand against Eddie's. "He's just lonely."

"We need to get off the ice," Steve pleaded. He started a slow walk towards her. The ice groaned beneath his feet, frigid water just inches away.

Then came the sound he'd been dreading. *Crack.*

The ice fractured into spiderwebs beneath his feet. He stopped dead and the cracks crawled outwards. Eddie smiled up at him from the lake. It wasn't a malicious smile. Just the smile of a child who was no longer alone.

"He just wanted someone to find his body," Lisa said as the cracks spread, and the ice gave way beneath them.

ALICE AUSTIN is an author of horror and fantasy – the weirder and creepier the better. She and her partner share their home in Kent, UK with an adorable menace of a cat. Find her on Twitter at @Al_Austin120

Beckwith House

Samantha Arthurs

The halls of Beckwith House came to life as the living themselves gave in to sleep, nestled deep into their beds as the snow continued to fall and was blown into tall drifts by the winds off the moor. Somewhere deep within the house a clock chimed the hour; it was late, sconces flickering to flame along the narrow corridors and inside the drafty ballroom. They did not use this room, not this time of year, but tonight the doors swung open to welcome back those who had previously departed.

Somehow, the house seemed to call out to them.

Welcome, welcome, ***welcome****.*

It was the music that woke the living; the sounds of a long-ago reverie echoing through the house. The children cowered beneath blankets, while the adults made sure that the doors were latched tight. No one would go downstairs, not until the sun had risen on Christmas morning and the spectral visitors who graced Beckwith House on every Eve were once again gone from this world.

They were never sure why the dead came back, choosing to partake in a long-ago party as though they were still part of the breathing world. Perhaps it was the joy of the Yuletide that drew them in, returning them to a place of good memories and camaraderie. Whatever it was it had always been so, the story passed down through generations of Beckwiths who came to live in the grand old house.

The fire crackled as the logs shifted on the grate, the children leaning in closer as Irving dropped his voice. It was the first year that his cousins were visiting for the holidays, and he felt it his duty to tell them the story of their ghostly visitors. He now pointed towards the clock that sat on the mantel. It read three minutes to midnight.

"They'll be here soon," he whispered to the others, eyeing them each in turn. "They're always on time."

Agatha shook her head, arms crossed defiantly over her chest. "It isn't true, and you know it! Father would never bring us to spend Christmas in a haunted house!"

"'Tis true," Irving bantered back at her, eyes narrowing. He did so detest to be called a liar. "Just you wait, Agatha! You ought not be calling folks liars!"

The children fell into an uneasy silence, the only sounds being their gentle breathing and the sounds of Beckwith House settling around them. The clock struck midnight, and for a moment it felt as though the house itself exhaled a long breath. Then, from downstairs, came the sounds of long-ago music and muted voices calling out to one another.

Agatha sat aghast as her siblings dove beneath the covers, looking at Irving who was the only one who did not seem afraid. Instead he merely shrugged his shoulders beneath his nightgown.

"I told you, Agatha. They always come home for Christmas."

SAMANTHA ARTHURS is the author of the Rust *series, the* Rag & Bone *trilogy, and the upcoming* Dreadful Seasons *series. You can read more about her and her stories at sarthurs.com.*

Hunger

Olivia Graves

The bell chimed midnight. A wheezing breath departed an exhausted pair of lungs, and with that the old master of the house was dead.

The doctor piled his stethoscope and needles and trays into his oversized black leather bag and snapped the metal clasp shut. He nodded to the servants. “Stop the clocks.”

A quiet calm descended upon the great house. Only the rustling of the leaves in the frigid winter air could be heard through the narrow window panes.

“Well,” said the butler, “good riddance.”

The doctor turned, astonished. “How’s that?”

“It’s nothing. Foolish talk around the kitchen fire.” A creak moved up the foundation of the house. “We always said he’d never walk again. Not if he made it past Christmas.”

"What do you mean," said the doctor, "'walk again'?"

The butler showed the doctor out the room and put the key in the lock. "What chime of the bell would you say he died at?" He seemed to hesitate, then he turned the key and slipped it under the door. "Never mind. Just in case."

"In case of what?" The doctor stumbled in his confusion and almost fell down the stairs.

"Careful! You don't want to stay here." The butler steadied the old doctor and led him safely to the foyer. Gently but firmly. "There, the coach will take you to the station. Best hurry. The train leaves a little early some nights."

The horses stirred beyond the front door. Clouds of steam billowed from their nostrils.

"But what did you mean?"

"Hurry!"

The door slammed shut and the doctor was left standing in the snow bank, watching the lights go out, one by one. There was no coach. No driver to take him away. Only the desolate road weaving into darkest night between the white hedgerows. He stepped back, stumbled against a lump of ice, and fell. He yelped. But it caught in his throat.

In the house moved a light, and the hand guiding it was monstrous and large and grasping. It was a shadow reaching, reaching through the bedroom window.

He screamed.

But there came no sound. Only the creaking of the trees, and a moaning in the wind, and a desperate sigh. A sigh of ravenous hunger. A hunger for his body and soul.

On this night, they say the great estate gained an amiable house doctor. And if you too should be called out to attend an aging master, or seal a drafty window, be sure you do not stay the night.

OLIVIA GRAVES is a Swedish trans writer of gothic horror and speculative fiction. Her writing often delves into existential terror and transformations both great and small. She has lived on two continents, has a deplorable lack of feline children, and would really like to catch a break every now and then. You can find Olivia on Twitter at @OliviaFiction.

Sea Grave

Danielle Edwards

The sea nymph screamed in fury, breaking through the surface of the water and spotting the object of her obsession in a lover's embrace. His hand rested lovingly on the red-haired beauty's pregnant belly. The seas rose in turmoil, mirroring her emotions, as jealous tears brought a torrential downpouring from the severed sky. Waves violently crashed over the deck as the couple tumbled into the sea, swallowed by its depths. In a final fit of rage, she tossed the woman's limp body onto the boat. It rolled across the deck, arms splaying out with every turn until she came to rest among frilly drenched garments spilling out from an elegant steamer trunk. With a violent shove, bones snapped, appendages protruded at unnatural angles, and the sea nymph locked the body within, separating the lovers forevermore.

A quiet hush had settled across the valley as snow blanketed the cobblestone streets. The soft glow of Christmas lights was slowly extinguishing as the townspeople retired to bed. Penny had been leaning against the frosted windowpane mesmerized by the sparkling magic of the moon reflecting off the snowflakes. Her sapphire eyes widened as she caught sight of a tiny flame high up on the hill. Blinking and rubbing her eyes, she squinted out through the wintry swirl until she spotted the light again. Perched over the village, the abandoned mansion's windows were being illuminated, one by one.

Snow scattered across the foyer tiles, almost reaching the grand staircase in the center as the blustering wind tangled her copper hair and threatened her lantern's flame. Everything was eerily silent. A chill raised the hairs on the back of her neck. Someone had lit a fire in the library hearth, and before it sat an old steamer trunk. A book with yellowed pages lay open beside it.

Penny felt a presence behind her. Whirling around, she was greeted by darkness. She shook her head and rubbed her arms.

"Stop being so silly," she murmured, approaching the fire.

Mitten tugged off, she knelt. Running her fingers across the weathered page, she had discovered the tragic sea tale.

Penny shifted to reach the steamer trunk lid. Her heart pounded within her chest as a cold sweat dampened her palms. The intricately fashioned metal felt like it was searing her skin. The hinges creaked in protest. Penny gasped as the empty eye sockets of a bleached skull stared up at her. A distorted skeleton was draped in a torn dress. The lid slammed shut as Penny stumbled backwards.

A sudden movement arrested her attention. Whipping to face the arching windows, she saw the heavy velvet curtains shifting. The ghost of a woman hovered in the silver moonlight. Her hand rested against her slender belly, and she pointed to the book. Penny followed her gaze and watched in awe as the pages turned. She glanced at the apparition, but she hadn't moved. The top line stole her breath.

He whispered against her ear, *"Let's call her Penny."*

As a child, DANIELLE EDWARDS could always be found curled up, reading a book. Now the mom of two energetic boys, wrangler of five cats, and a physical therapist assistant for little friends with special needs, she gives her spare time to bleeding her heart out on the page. Find her on Twitter @dovetale5

Laid Out in Lavender

Leila Martin

He lays me out on satin. It's cool; whispers under my weight. Might even be comfy, but I'm rigid as a willow branch. He brushes away a fly twitching across my brow, opens a little pot, dips his fingertips in it and brings them out bloody. He dabs 'em over my lips.

This dress is too fancy for me, but I got to admit I do like lavender blue. 'S regal, innit? Like the song. It's starched stiff as I am, pleats pinned in place, neat as you like. There's lace at my throat too, foaming thick as baby's breath.

You'd say, I'm sure, this is too much pomp for a silly girl. Was I too friendly, as the papers would 'ave it? Should I 'ave been savvy, and seen through your disguise?

Too late, I saw your smile turn savage; felt your fingers' iron grip. Constellations of broken glass spun in the lamp-light an' 'fore I could shout my head cracked the cobbles, and above us the moon cut a sickle in the crushed-velvet sky an' your blade flashed, and I glimpsed a face reflected there that wasn't my own no more.

Christ. That wild mask will haunt me 'til the end of days.

S'pose you read in the papers: I nearly made it long enough to tell. Hope that gave you a fright. I came home blossoming crimson, reeling a two-step, the world stretching and shrinking like it was pulled through bellows. The night sank into the clink of the iodine bottle, the whirr of bandages. Swampy waves of pain, and then. At last. Brittle numbness creeping over me with the dawn.

Look: he's tied up some posies with ribbons and bows. Pretty, 'aint they? One by one, he tucks 'em beside me. *Sleep now*, he says. He closes my eyelids.

I tell yer', the smell of them's a relief. It'll sweeten my dreams.

What shall I dream of now? Shall I dream of him?

He could 'ave hummed a saccharine tune as he worked; he could 'ave ignored my rips. After all, who would see? But he's a *gentleman*, and he stitched me back together. He's everything you 'aint.

I won't come for him when I open my milky eyes and steal from this luxury box, intent as a desperate lie, spooling my pastel threads through the damp twilight an' over those glittering cobbles. Wafting my heady, floral-scented dreams thick as crinolines through an open window.

Can you smell the lavender yet?

We will dream together, you and I. You—and only you—will feel my cool skin press against yours. You will feel the thorny bristle of my stitches. I'll grip your face hard in my marbled hands. I'll give us back all the years you so gleefully plucked from me, and more besides.

Hush, now. I'll sew your scream silent. Listen to the whoosh of the needle and thread.

I'm gonna make you a mask of your own.

LEILA MARTIN is a writer from Manchester, where she shares a small house with a small number of people and a tremendous number of books. Her stories have appeared in Fireside Magazine, Cossmass Infinities *and* Daily Science Fiction. *You can find her on Twitter @Bookishleels.*

Sister Agnes

H.B. Diaz

Sister Agnes was dead to begin with. Let there be no doubt whatever about that. This fact must be understood before we can introduce young Mr. Sorrell, a man of few prospects and fewer friends, who found himself without engagement this Christmas Eve. The deacon had locked up the church after evening mass. Sorrell's cousin, who lived in a cottage on the hill, turned him away, as did the inn keeper, for there were no more rooms to let. In a threadbare coat soaked by snow, his wanderings led him at last to the gates of Briar Abbey.

The skeletal figures of oak and yew flanked the pebble drive, sentinels in the frozen night. He paid no mind to the legend as he heaved open the bleeding iron door and stepped inside. The specter of Sister Agnes, fated for all eternity to grieve her lost lover, frightened him less than the thought of spending the night out in the cold.

Sorrell's footsteps scattered rats and shadows alike across the narthex, the naked moon gleaming like silver on the debris-strewn floor. He settled down in the corner of this liminal space with a stake of holly in his heart.

As he shivered, nearly napping, he felt the gentle touch of a woman's hand upon his cheek. With a hideous cry, he shrunk back against the stones. Raw flesh and weeping blisters knotted together to form her face. Sunken eyes peered at him from beneath her veil, and her mouth cracked apart in a curious expression of recognition.

William, she spoke, though her disfigured lips did not move.

He did not correct her, for his heart was touched. Her fingers landed upon his breast, and he knew her at once. She bestowed upon him all that had befallen her, and he saw it as clearly as a memory.

"She killed your lover," he whispered. "The abbess. She pushed him from the library window."

She found us that night in the cloister, Agnes answered, her head listing to one side. *You had to be punished.*

"Your face," he muttered. Deep inside his mind, he watched the abbess lift a pot of boiling water and cast its wretched contents into Sister Agnes' face. Seared skin slipped down over her jaw, exposing the muscle beneath, her scream so ghastly that he covered his ears.

My beauty was a sin, she said, drawing him back. *I am pure now.*

With pity in his heart, Sorrell reached for her, and he saw her as she once was. The ruined skin stretched across her cheeks like a bolt of silk, leaving behind only the blush of passion. Locks of golden hair tumbled down over her wrinkled habit, full lips parting softly to speak.

I have been waiting for you a long time, William.

"I am here," he answered, but he did not know his own voice.

H.B. DIAZ is a gothic mystery writer whose short stories have appeared in publications by Ghost Orchid Press, Flame Tree Press, The NoSleep Podcast, and others. Her gothic romance novel, The Ghost of Ravenswood Hall, *is forthcoming from Literary Wanderlust. She is a member of the Horror Writers Association and lives with her family in a historic and likely haunted town on America's east coast. You can find her on Twitter @hollybdiaz or Instagram @h.b.diaz.*

The Bodegraven Man

Clyde Davis

Out in the highlands—where heath meets hearth, where the grey clouds inhabit the few who call this wilderness home—there are few occasions to dispel the cold-hearted, to banish the desolate woes roaming the rolling hills. Out in the highlands, beneath the ominous tones and tundra tides, Christmas Eve is held close, like a precious jewel against the winter dark.

Candles are lit and lanterns line the cobbled streets, whilst tinsel festoons the stony walls of the croft cottage rows. The villages shed their dreary skin, and for one night, the weathered folk of the north allow cheer into their hearts, and reacquaint themselves with its forgotten friend, laughter. Trees are felled and trimmed, erected beneath thatched roofs and decorated with wooden baubles and sculpted cones. As the evening falls, fires spring to life and crackle like amber glass; the running colours spilling through the night, pouring through splintered shutters and roughened doors. Families congregate to feast on venison stew; the deep taste of mountain herbs sits subtly on their tongues, and the bitter embrace of ale coils around their teeth. Bread is broken, and merriment shared. Tarts are cut, and memories handed down. Eggnog is sipped, and stories told. Out in the highlands, these are the rituals of Christmas Eve. The rites of joyful souls.

Yet, there is one tale never muttered about the festive table. A tale hardly told, for each word is true. It is the tale of the Bodegraven Man. As the cheer is churned and laughter echoes through streets, the Bodegraven Man is called down from the hills. From all the light his shadow is cast, and down he lopes, naked legs and sagging skin, towards the villages, towards the homes. But in the darkness he won't be found, for he skulks in through the shadows, and stands behind the Christmas tree. There he waits, the old wrinkled suit of pale flesh. His long hands fiddle behind the leaves, his sour breath whistles through crooked teeth, and saucer eyes black as hellish night, crowned by red rings, stare through unblinking lids. There he waits, and watches the families feast. A wretched tongue licks his lips, while he looks for the saddest one. Despite the merriment and hallow songs, the Bodegraven Man knows, there is always a heavy heart, or a secret kept, a gloomy soul unsatisfied. He has come for them, and when the fires burn down, he will come out from behind the tree, and creep towards the beds of the unhappy ones. There, he will have his own merry feast. Blood and marrow, bone and grits, hair and nails, sometimes even the pillow slips.

The Bodegraven Man. He is always there, standing behind the Christmas tree, watching and waiting. No one tells the tale, and no one looks, but if you pause, you may catch a glimpse of his fetid skin peeping through the evergreen, and if you listen, you'll hear his creaking bones beneath the chilly highland winds.

CLYDE DAVIS is an author of gothic, dark fantasy, horror and speculative fiction. He currently manages a weekly flash fiction newsletter titled Narrativ, *and his debut novel,* Blackwood, *is currently being produced into a podcast series. Clyde currently resides in the Netherlands, where he is working on his sophomore novel.*

Links:
Narrativ: https://narrativ.substack.com/about
Blackwood, A Gotheim Tale: https://amzn.to/2GsU8LN
Twitter: https://twitter.com/_ClydeDavis

Also Available from Ghost Orchid Press

ghostorchidpress.com

Made in the USA
Las Vegas, NV
29 November 2024